THE TALE OF THE LOST BALLOON

Story told by Guido-Burrito
Interpreted by Author: Marilyn Cummins
Illustrated by Artist: Carol White
Published by: Nine Tails Adventures,
Lawrenceville, GA 30046 USA

Carol White

Marilyn Cummins

Library of Congress control Number: 2019903981

ISBN: 978-1-7923-0726-3

I.   Title: THE TALE of the LOST BALLOON
(Book 1 of 9)
II. Author: Cummins, Marilyn
Illustrator: White, Carol
III. Subject: Humorous dog adventures — Fiction
Illustrated Children's chapter book — Fiction
Summary: Book 1 — 9 dogs embark on a walk in the woods and they stumble
In and out of 5 zany adventures.

This is **a read-together book** for ages from 4-94 to share and enjoy.
Type-face — interior: Franklin Gothic Book 14-24 pt.
Illustrations: acrylic wash with pen and ink

Published by: Nine Tails Adventures, Lawrenceville, GA. USA
www.ninetailsadventures.com

Printed on FSC (Forest Stewardship Council approved) paper
Using Chlorine free inks (acid free)
Made in the USA

Contents

Notes from

Guido-Burrito...

For this Read-together book.

For Parents:

Encourage your young reader to look up new words in the Glossary.

For Young Readers:

Don't know the meaning of a word? Look it up in the Glossary on pages 71, 72.

Match up the 9 dogs to their gifts with the Fun Puzzle #1 on page 67.

Find the Magic Word hidden in the Puzzle #2 on page 68.

5 fun chapter adventures. Enjoy the story together...

Reading is fun.

Chapter 1

THE ESCAPE

"I wish I had wings and could fly," I day-dreamed on the first brilliant and bedazzling spring day of the year. I'd spent the morning lounging on my cushion-by-the-window, safely snuggled in the sunlight.

I am always the first in my family to bounce from bed, tumble and twirl for treats and trill with the radio to cheer my two-paw pals as they leave for work or school.

This is my job, you see, I am Guido-Burrito, The Gracious Greeter. I know how to make every meeting a celebration — even if you're only gone two minutes!

Maybe it was hearing the blissful buzzing of bees as they

bounded from dahlia to daffodil, or the scent of mushrooms and moss and mud, or frogs and flies and flocks of fowl that was making me restless. I knew that this was the perfect day for exploring the park with my fur friends.

(I should warn you that I really like repeating sounds like *bbb* and *ddd* and *sss* as my trademark bark.)

Allow me to introduce the Nine Tail Adventurers:

Tara, Duncan, Sophia

Gabby, Julie, Me, Murphy

Lord Gray, and Sir Hamil

Each of my
friends
has a special
escape plan.

Meet our 9 Tails Adventurers

Tara rolls

Duncan cleans

Sophia ponders

Gabby bounces

Julie poses

Guido barks

Murphy hides

Having Fun!

Lord Gray considers

Sir Hamil watches

To escape, I needed to carefully slide into my boy's backpack and
jump out as he passed the park entrance on his way to school.

Lord Gray stands on top of Sir Hamil to reach the key stored above the door frame.

Gabby shows Duncan and Julie how to push the fence boards and squeeze through.

Tara tips over a water bucket to show Sophia and Murphy
the big hole she dug under the fence.

Finally together, our ordinary woodsy romp quickly turned into an adventure. We followed our noses, marching down the trail, sneaking past the picnic area and into the wilds.

Then, in a clearing , Murphy spotted **IT:** a magical, mysterious menace moving in the meadow.

"**It** looks like a pair of gorilla's knickers," said Sir Hamil to Lord Gray, the Dignified Dane from Dusseldorf.

"**It's** a bride's veil," chimed Tara, our tenacious terrier.
"**It** wiggles, sparkles and squeaks!" cheered the girls of gold.
"**It's** a toy !" they agreed.
"Maybe we should just watch **it** for a minute to see what **it** does before we fetch **it**," warned Duncan and Sophia, our wise and cautious friends.

But their warning was too late: Murphy and I were already sniffing the tie-downs and jumping into the gondola to see what was inside.

"It is plain to the eye
That it fell from the sky.
Not the jumbo pantaloons
Of a hairy baboon —
IT'S A SCIENCE BALLOON"

cried Murphy, who liked to speak in rhymes.

just then.....

And this is how Murphy and I
became accidental aviators.
My Mother told me to be careful what I wished for.

Chapter 2

THE BIG TOP

The Balloon shot Skyward...

then twisted

and twirled, curled and unfurled, wiggled and whirled.

But all of the tugging by Tara, Duncan, and the golden girls couldn't stop the balloon from careening away with Murphy and me onboard.

"Oh! No! The wind is blowing faster than we can run," warned the Great Danes. "Soon we won't be able to see them in the sky and look: there's a river."

"Don't worry. We're bird dogs: we can see small objects flying in the sky. And a RIVER, oh boy! Splashing, swimming, getting wet and slimy. That's the life!" replied Julie, bristling with joy.

"Ahem. We will cross at the bridge," the Danes said with great dignity. "We are guardians of the nobility, or so the legend goes. With no princes and princesses here, we'll just have to guard all of you."

"Look," Tara said, "Guido and Murphy are throwing things over the side of the balloon and leaving a trail. I can track anything on the ground."

"Me, too," added Duncan.

"Rabbits, squirrels, chipmunks, or this plastic gizmo."

"This bluster is blowing us briskly backwards into a BIG TOP," I warned.

> "When we blow thru the flaps
> We should tug on these straps,
> Make the airbag collapse....
> And then, just perhaps
> We can exit this trap,"

answered Murphy.

"Hey!" yelled Lord Gray as he lifted the plastic object Duncan found. "These 2-way radios are for communication between the ground crew and the balloon. This must have been used by scientists, or weathermen, or SPIES!

If we can get one of these back to Guido and Murphy, we'll be able to talk to our fly boys and won't lose them."

"I can do it," Tara bravely and proudly announced as she grabbed the headset and launched herself toward a trampoline net inside the tent.

You see, Tara didn't like tall things like trees or cliffs or buildings, so she especially wouldn't like riding in a balloon. But she was courageous and would overcome her fears to help her friends.

"Tara, you tumble the trapeze like a trouper" I proclaimed.

"While your air spins were splendid
As your feet were suspended.
We admire your style
And your sweet, brave smile,
But bringing that headset
Is the best luck we've had yet," quipped Murphy.

Then WHOOOOOSH.........

They were blown out the other side of the tent.

"Oh, No, NO, NO.

I don't do air.
I'm Tara. TARA , the Terrier.
Get It?
Tara/Terrier/Terra
Firma/Land/Dirt"
I chase small animals into tunnels.
Tunnels in dirt.

GET ME BACK ON THE GROUND!!!!!"

Chapter 3

THE VIRTUE OF VULTURES

"**Murphy,** be really calm so we don't terrify Tara, but check out the characters cavorting behind us,"
I whispered.

"**Uh, Oh!**

They plunge and plummet

From sewer to summit,

Scouring the ground

For a road-kill McNugget!"

Murphy joked as we watched a large squadron of vultures spiral around our balloon.

"**WOW!** Look at the flock of eagles," Tara said as she waved for the birds to approach the balloon.

"Oh, Mister Eagle,

I need to get down there," she pleaded, pointing toward the ground. "Can you give me a ride?"

"Why no, little Miss,

I can't. Your weight is too much for my wings to support. But you can hitch a ride on our Bone Drone if one of your friends can handle the controller," the scruffy but sympathetic vulture replied.

"Allow me to introduce

myself. I am Vince, The Vice-Admiral of Vultures.

My friends just call me Vinnie," he said as he tipped his head and saluted with one wing.

"You really have a drone?" I asked, suddenly interested in the bad-breath bird. Technology has always been one of my favorite hobbies. I enjoyed chewing cell phones and burying remote controllers during my puppy years. Lately, barking at Siri has captured my attention.

"Yup. My flight crew and I have a huge territory to search to locate our dinner. That means we are always tired.......and always hungry. We all have keen eyesight, but sometimes we just can't spot carrion, or I mean a carrot," he declared as he preened his chest feathers.

"**One day** the crew and I were resting in a dead tree when we spotted this strange-looking bird stuck high in the branches. It was buzzing like a humming-bird while this featherless stork-looking being jumped up and down and squawked at us to *get away from his drone.*"

"**Well,** we were all too tired to fly, too curious about the health of that buzzing thing and too annoyed by the squawker, so we dropped our heads and flapped our wings. That made the man throw down the controller and run for his car.

We like cars, they are our best friends!"

"Herman over there, dropped down and snatched the controller while the rest of us freed the drone from the branches."

"We all agreed that the drone didn't look natural, so we camouflaged it with old bones and feathers. Then we taught ourselves how to work the controller and camera and started using it to scout for our food. See, the camera scans our territory for uhhhh......carcass cuisine, you might say, and when it spots a meal we just fly to the coordinates."

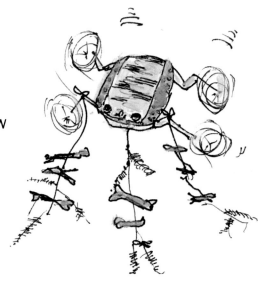

"My crew now has time for hobbies and even charity work. Reggie learned the art of making sushi, and Norm knits blankets out of hair for our nests.

We all volunteer for

Keep America Beautiful — the roadside clean-up detail, because of our special talents, if you know what I mean," he finished, laughing and winking at us.

"**See that trio** of butter-colored dogs below us?" Tara asked, pointing at Gabby, Julie and Sophia. "They are hunting dogs born to retrieve almost anything. If you give them that controller they can retrieve ME!"

Instantly, Vinnie flew down to the gathering of dogs and passed the controller to Julie while Lord Gray, Sir Hamil and Duncan watched from behind a large rock. Needless to say, they looked quite confused, but I think they were adjusting to this rather unusual day.

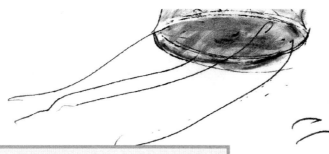

With a few instructions from Vinnie, the girls were able to fly the Bone Drone skyward to retrieve Tara, who leaped onto a bone dangling from the bottom.

Being the tricksters they naturally are, the girls couldn't resist twisting and turning the levers to make the drone do loops and spins. Poor Tara hung on for her life.

"Give that controller to me, NOW," demanded Lord Gray as he snatched the Instrument away from the girls and brought poor Tara safely back to earth.

Sir Hamil then took the controller, holding it over his head, as Vinnie, Vice-Admiral of Vultures, swerved to grab it with his talons.

Then the Danes saluted and thanked the vultures for their virtue.

"Glad to be of help.

Stay off the roads," he laughed as

the gang of birds flew away.

Chapter 4

This was not a typical trail trek for me or my pals, I thought as I viewed the lakes, dams, fields and orchards passing below. This is a genuine caper; an adventure that challenges all of our talents and skills.

"Hey Murphy. Why are you shaking?" I asked, noticing that Murphy had a tight grasp on the gondola's edge.

> **"Vultures that spy.**
>
> **Tara spinning in the sky.**
>
> **Tents full of tigers,**
>
> **And now pigs that can fly!"**

Murphy exclaimed as he pointed downward toward a dense cornfield surrounded by towering silos, barns, pens and clapping crowds of children.

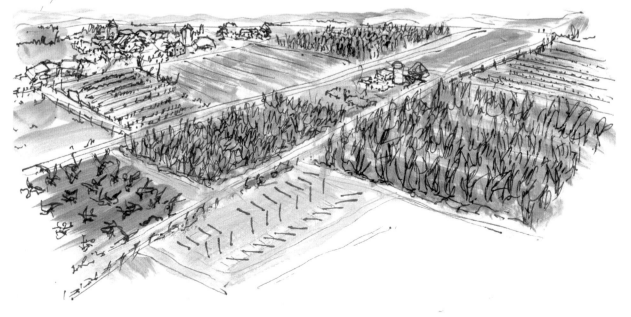

"It's Farmer Jim's Maze-Craze-Daze. That pirouetting pig poses for pin-up pictures for people," I said, pleased with my perfect perceptions.

"And one just pranced his pudgy pork chops out of his pen," I added.

From our perch-in-the-sky we could see the pig fly over fences as he raced headlong toward the corn maze with Farmer Jim and two petite pigs in pursuit.

Inside the maze we could see a mom pushing a stroller while a small child, concentrating on his game-boy, lagged behind. Murphy and I watched as the mom turned right in the maze while the boy turned left and into the path of the approaching pig.

"Oh, no! He'll get lost —
or worse, pulverized by the pig,"
I yelled. "I'll use the radio to alert
Sir Hamil and the gang. .
They can save the boy."

 Sir Hamil and Lord Gray quickly organized a plan: they would chase the pig, just as their ancestors had hunted for wild boar. Duncan and Tara, the tracking terriers, would follow the boy by his scent. Gabby, Julie and Sophia were directed to fetch the mom and her baby.

WHEN SUDDENLLY THE BOY DISAPPEARED!

As Murphy and I frantically scanned the scene below, we could see the pig racing toward a huge pile of acorns. He dove into the pile and used his snout as a shovel to dig through the nuts.

CORN MAZE

Just then Sir Hamil and Lord Gray burst through a corn row while Duncan and Tara ran closely behind.

This persistent pig ignored all of their barking and continued

doggedly digging into the pile. A foot suddenly emerged, then part of a leg.

And that is when all the dogs joined in, scattering acorns into the

air as they worked.

Lord Gray used his muzzle to gently push the boy out of the pile. Then he and Sir Hamil surrounded the wheezing child, keeping him safe from the unpredictable pig.

Suddenly, the wind shifted and our balloon plummeted, dropping Murphy and me muzzle-to-snout with the ponderous pig.

"Hey, there," I said with bravado (while my heart wildly pounded). "I'm Guido-Burrito, the Gracious Greeter. I am a chivalrous and courageous bull-fighting Chihuahua. You are only a surly swine, smaller and so less savage than a bull. I will bravely battle for the boy you are badgering."

To my surprise, the pig bowed, tipped his head and said:

"Ola, mi amigo! Yo soy—that is, I am—a proud Iberian pig from Spain, the home of bull fighting. Farmer Jim stores these acorns for my food."

"I wasn't chasing the boy to harm him, I wanted his mango snack."

"I'm crazy for mangos. They are much tastier than acorns. In fact they call me Senor Mango Fandango, the Spanish-speaking, mango eating, flamenco dancing pig," he explained.

Just then, an out-of-breath Farmer Jim and two more pigs entered the clearing while Gabby, Julie and Sophia led the boy's mother toward the group.

"Allow me to introduce my wife, Tango Fandango, and son, Durango Fandango. We all entertain the crowds with Spanish dancing during Maze Craze Daze."

And just when Murphy and I thought that we too, were rescued and safely on the ground, a blasting breeze blew us back into the blue........once again leaving our friends far below.

Chapter 5

The Fire

" Now there's a pig that would squeal
    With joy and great zeal——
    Not for saving a child,
    But for stealing his meal,"
Murphy rhymed while high-fouring me for
my important role in the boy's rescue.

"We shall siesta as we sashay across a sapphire
sky," I announced. Except the sky wasn't a
gemstone blue, it was boiling in big black billows
blasting upward from our park.

"The park is on fire!" I screamed into the radio.

"Hurry Sir Ham, hurry Lord Gray. Call the rangers and alert
them to the disaster, then put the Nine Tails to work."

While the dependable Danes directed, the terriers trenched, and retrievers rescued, Murphy and I did air reconnaissance.

"Hurry gang," I cautioned, "The fire is moving faster then we Nine Tails can fight it! We need help, **NOW!**"

And just then the sky shaded as a squadron of vultures led by Vice-Admiral Vinnie and the Bone-Drone flew past our balloon. Each vulture was equipped with a water-filled bucket held in his talons.   On the ground I could see Mango, Tango, and Durango Fandango sprinting with Farmer Jim toward the park. Behind this group of Maize-Craze strays was a circus troupe of volunteers:

Goats pulling boats,
Acrobats with vats,
Clowns squirting water from crowns,
Tigers with tails twisted around pails
And an entire dancing-horse work-force!

"Look up there," I said, pointing toward a lone circling vulture. "It's Vinnie with the bone-drone."

"Please help me," he pleaded. "My nest is burned and all the eggs are gone. I have to find my family."

"Don't worry, our friend," the darling little Duncan soothed, "just ask Gabby to smile."

...and Gabby smiled, exposing three beautiful vulture eggs cradled safely in her mouth.

"**We did it!** We saved our park!,"
I triumphantly proclaimed, jumping
for joy as the rangers arrived to find
an extinguished fire and an
exhausted assortment of dogs,
hogs, squirrels floating on logs, and
circus performers in charred togs.

"Guido! Don't hop!
Our balloon will pop.
The Park tower's on the right
And we may end this flight
By crashing on its top!" warned Murphy

And that is just what happened; we
slammed into the tower with a huge
hiss and a thud——sending Murphy
and me catapulting onto the catwalk.

...where we were greeted by our Nine-Tails brothers and sisters.

What a strange and wonderful team we made: each a different size and color, some with long limbs, some short; some good at swims, some good at sports; one that trots, one that dashes; one with spots, one with long eyelashes; some ears dropped, some cropped. Yet we were dogs, one and all, each with special talents that contributed toward solving problems that we could not do alone.

Guido tells us...

We all learned that diversity

Doesn't come from our looks, you see;

Not from the length of our muzzle

Or how long tongues help us guzzle,

Not the wag of our tails

Or whiskers and toenails...

Vinnie Ventures...

It's not the hook in our beaks
Or fine-feathered physiques,
Nor our noble profession
With its outlaw impression...

Fandango family finds...

It's not a tail that can kink
Or a snout that turns pink
Nor a smelly slop meal
That to most won't appeal...

Circus concludes...

It's not a jaw full of teeth
Or a striped underneath,
Nor a loud scary roar,
Or horns that can gore...

It's the gifts we share

with joy and great flair

that make the world better

'cause we're stronger *together*.

The Tale End

Our next adventure bears reading....

FUN WORD PUZZLE #1

The Match-Up

The 9 Tails Adventurers are pictured on the right and left margins of this puzzle page.

Can you identify them? On the line in List 1 enter the number of the word that <u>you</u> think best describes each dog in List 2.

If you are not sure, check the story again for hints. To check your answers turn to the bottom of page 69.

Give it a try and have fun.

List 1		List 2	
Duncan	____	Dependable	1
Gabby	____	Brave	2
Guido-Burrito	____	Poet	3
Julie	____	Wise	4
Sir Hamil	____	Joyous	5
Lord Gray	____	Greeter	6
Murphy	____	Dignified	7
Sophia	____	Darling	8
Tara	____	Trickster	9

FUN WORD PUZZLE #2

The Secret Word

Find 18 words from the story in the yellow box...and discover the Secret Word

Instructions:

1.) first find each word from the Word List at the bottom of the page.

2.) Then circle the letters as we have done with the word "net" and cross them off your list.

Hint #1: words can appear up, down, and sideways, or even backwards, so keep searching...

Hint #2: some letters can be used more than once, so don't cover them up so you can't read them...

3.) When you have circled all letters in all 18 words, you will see that there are 8 letters without circles.

4.) Write them down in the order they appear top--to—bottom in the blue box below.

To check your word, turn to the bottom of page 70.

C	I	R	C	U	S	D	A	M
0	L	R	T	R	I	R	P	R
R	0	O	G	E	L	O	A	A
N	E	T	U	L	O	N	L	F
M	G	S	E	D	S	E	F	R
A	D	E	E	D	S	T	I	I
Z	I	C	K	O	H	E	R	V
E	R	N	A	T	R	A	E	E
R	B	A	L	L	O	O	N	R

18 story word List

ART	CORN	LAKE
ANCESTOR	DAM	NET
BALLOON	DRONE	MAZE
BRIDGE	FARM	RIVER
CIRCUS	FIRE	SILOS
CLOUDS	FLAP	TODDLER

Magic Word entered here...

_

_____

68

Dedication

This fun romp is dedicated to all the playful spirits of our dear dog friends.

Dogs have boundless love for us even when we are cranky or too busy. If we will slow down and stop mindlessly pushing forward, that shared love is magnified and returned many times over.

Listed below are the dogs in our lives who have shared their gifts and love.

Marilyn

"Brandy", "Solo" and "Fidget", wire-haired Fox Terriers

"Murphy", confection of anonymous and Chinese Crested sources

"Sophia" yellow Lab and Golden mix

"Duncan", white West Highland Terrier

"Guilie (Julie)" and "Gabby", Golden Retrievers, sisters

Carol

"Princess", black Retriever mix

"Onyx", black German Shepherd

"Kelly", black Cocker Spaniel

"Boo-boo", Cocker-Poo, son of Kelly

"Tara III", wire-haired Fox Terrier

"Jennie Churchill", Blenheim Cavalier King Charles Spaniel

And special thanks to our dear friend John Dolphy for allowing us to co-star his two beautiful Great Danes; "Greystone" and "Hamilton", brothers.

Our suggested answer: 8-9-6-5-1-7-3-4-2

Biographical

Author: Marilyn Cummins

Photo by Carol White

Location: L' Isle Sur La Sorgue, France

Illustrator: Carol White

Photo by Carol White

Location: Bellagio on Lake Como, Italy

In the beginning there was the word.

And the word was.....BALL

With one word we establish dialogue between two very different species, and very rapidly the conversations expand: "sit, stay, come, don't eat the flowers, the hose is not a snake, chew your toy, not my shoes," and on and on until you find yourself spelling out words to avoid riots:

"c-o-o-k-l-e, p-a-r-k, v-e-t".

Because they possess an unmatched willingness of spirit and the most open of pure hearts, dogs learn how to joyfully navigate through the complex and un-dog-ish modern world. If we are half as smart, we learn or re-learn that there is jumping joy in tall grasses, bliss and wonder in the woods, and that there is always one person in a crowd dropping cookie crumbs.

I wanted to spend the rest of my life learning the secrets of happiness from dogs, so I closed my business and with the encouragement of a dear friend, embarked on writing this dog adventure. This friend is the book's fabulous illustrator, Carol White. She thinks I have an active inner-child—I hope it's really an inner-dog!

Marilyn and I both love animals;

especially dogs

I knew this book would be a fun project for the both of us, and I knew Marilyn was the right person to write the storyline. She came up with some great adventures...this is her gift to share...a delightful and entertaining imagination.

I'm 'drawing' from my life's experience of bringing up kids and mothering dogs. My art education started with BFA degree from Massachusetts College of Art and Design, Boston. Post graduate work in Art Education brought me into the classroom for another perspective of children and young adults.

We have imbued our nine very different dogs with gifts solving their various challenges that we felt would appeal to parents reading to children, as well as young readers themselves.

The animal world is amazing in its diversity and beauty. For us, dogs hold a very special place in that world. Their unconditional love and forgiveness of us is unparalleled for which we are very grateful.

Secret word: Together

GLOSSARY

Accidental: happening by chance

Aviators: pilots

Bedazzle: greatly impressive, sparkling

Bellow: emit deep, loud roar

Big Top: main tent in a circus

Bravado: boldness

Camouflaged: disguised or hidden

Careening: move swiftly in an uncontrolled way

Carrion: decaying flesh, dead animals

Catapult: to hurl or throw

Catwalk: narrow passageway

Cavalier: dashing, casual

Coordinates: positions, locations

Courageous: brave, fearless

Cuisine: style of eating or cooking

Doggedly: persistent, determined

Dusseldorf: town in Germany

Flamenco: spirited Spanish dancing

Frantically: hurried, excited

Glossary: a list of difficult words with definitions

Gondola: compartment hanging below balloon

GLOSSARY CONTINUED

Gracious: pleasant, tactful

Iberian: peninsula of land forming Spain and Portugal

Knickers: underwear

Maze: complex network of paths

Menace: threat or danger

Nobility: aristocrats, people with inherited titles

Pantaloons: long, frilly undergarments

Perceptions: understanding or awareness of something

Persistent: determined

Pirouetting: twirling and whirling

Plummet: drop straight downward

Ponderous: slow because of great weight

Reconnaissance: observation to learn important information

Sashay: walking swinging your hips

Squadron: group of flying things

Sympathetic: supportive, comforting

Talons: claw on bird of prey

Terra Firma: solid ground

Troupe: group of entertainers

Unpredictable: behaving in a way that you can't guess

Virtue: behavior showing high moral standards

74

Made in the USA
Columbia, SC
15 May 2019